HOW TO DRAW YOUR OWN GRAPHIC NOVEL

CREATING THE COVER FOR YOUR GRAPHIC NOVEL

FRANK LEE

PowerKiDS press™

New York

Published in 2012 by The Rosen Publishing Group, Inc.

29 East 21st Street, New York, NY 10010

Text and Illustrations: Frank Lee with Peter Gray

Editors: Joe Harris and Kate Overy

U.S. Editor: Kara Murray

Design: Andrew Easton

Cover Design: Andrew Easton

Library of Congress Cataloging-in-Publication Data

Lee, Frank, 1980—

Creating the cover for your graphic novel / by Frank Lee.

        p. cm. — (How to draw your own graphic novel)

Includes index.

ISBN 978-1-4488-6436-2 (library binding) — ISBN 978-1-4488-6457-7 (pbk.) —

ISBN 978-1-4488-6458-4 (6-pack)

1. Comic book covers—Juvenile literature. 2. Comic books, strips, etc.—Technique—Juvenile literature.

3. Graphic novels—Juvenile literature. I. Title.

NC974.L44 2012

741.5′1—dc23

                        2011030630

Printed in China

SL002067US

CPSIA Compliance Information: Batch #AW2102PK: For Further Information contact Rosen Publishing, New York, New York at 1-800-237-9932

CONTENTS

Drawing Tools...4

The Classic Hero Cover...6

The Story Cover...12

The Teaser Cover...18

Horror and Manga Covers..24

Glossary...30

Further Reading...31

Web Sites...31

Index...32

DRAWING TOOLS

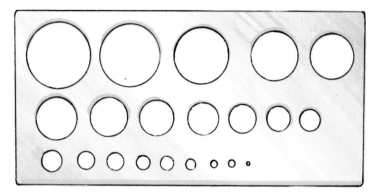

CIRCLE TEMPLATE
This is very useful for drawing small circles.

LAYOUT PAPER
Most professional illustrators use cheaper paper for basic layouts and practice sketches before they get around to the more serious task of producing a masterpiece on more costly paper. It's a good idea to buy some plain paper from a stationery shop for all of your practice sketches. Go for the least expensive kind.

DRAWING PAPER
This is a heavy-duty, high-quality paper, ideal for your final version. You don't have to buy the most expensive brand. Most decent art or craft shops stock their own brand or a student brand and, unless you're thinking of turning professional, these will do fine.

WATERCOLOR PAPER
This paper is made from 100 percent cotton and is much higher quality than wood-based papers. Most art shops stock a large range of weights and sizes. Paper that is 140 pounds (300 g/m) should be fine.

FRENCH CURVES
These are available in a few shapes and sizes and are useful for drawing curves.

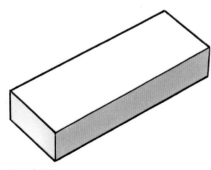

ERASER
There are three main types of eraser: rubber, plastic, and putty. Try all three to see which kind you prefer.

PENCILS

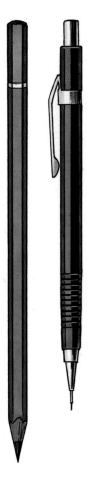

It's best not to cut corners on quality here. Get a good range of graphite (lead) pencils ranging from soft (#1) to hard (#4).

Hard lead lasts longer and leaves less graphite on the paper. Soft lead leaves more lead on the paper and wears down more quickly. Every artist has their personal preference, but #3 pencils are a good medium range to start out with until you find your favorite.

Spend some time drawing with each weight of pencil and get used to their different qualities. Another good product to try is the mechanical pencil. These are available in a range of lead thicknesses, 0.5 mm being a good medium range. These pencils are very good for fine detail work.

PENS

There is a large range of good-quality pens on the market these days and all will do a decent job of inking. It's important to experiment with different pens to determine which you are most comfortable using.

You may find that you end up using a combination of pens to produce your finished artwork. Remember to use a pen that has waterproof ink if you want to color your illustration with a watercolor or ink wash. It's a good idea to use one of these anyway. There's nothing worse than having your nicely inked drawing ruined by an accidental drop of water!

BRUSHES

Some artists like to use a fine brush for inking linework. This takes a bit more practice and patience to master, but the results can be very satisfying. If you want to try your hand at brushwork, you will definitely need to get some good-quality sable brushes.

These are very versatile pens and, with practice, can give pleasing results.

INKS

With the dawn of computers and digital illustration, materials such as inks have become a bit obscure, so you may have to look harder for these. Most good art and craft shops should stock them, though.

THE CLASSIC HERO COVER

JUDGING A BOOK BY ITS COVER

The most important part of a comic book is its cover. The design and artwork of a cover must grab the interest of a potential reader. In this guide we'll introduce you to several different approaches to cover creation. The first of these is the classic, iconic hero cover, which shows the lead character in a dynamic pose.

STEP 1: ROUGHS

The first stage of the design process is the creation of thumbnail roughs. These are small, simple sketches and layouts of potential cover designs.

FIRST ROUGH

In this example, the hero, Omegaman, is standing on a rooftop, surveying the city. We can immediately tell he is strong, brave, and ready for action. This type of cover design is often used for first issue covers.

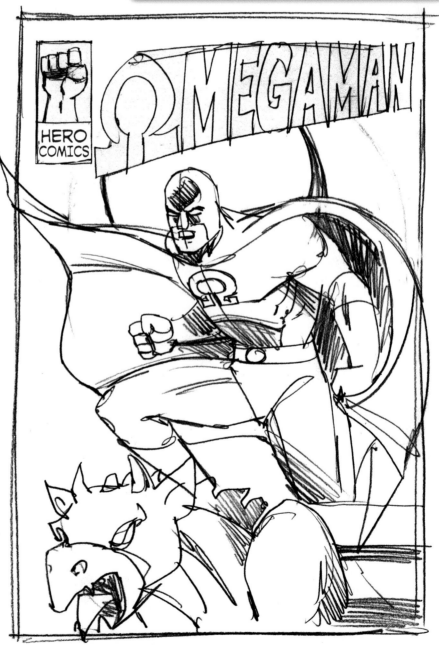

SECOND ROUGH

This second attempt at a cover design shows our lead character looking nobly into the distance, with the moon looming behind him. The gargoyle has been dropped from the bottom of the image.

STEP 2: PENCILS

Now we need to choose the most effective elements from each rough to use on the final cover. We've chosen to keep the gargoyle from the first rough. We've taken the upright pose from the second rough, as well as the use of the moon as a framing device.

STEP 3: INKS

Once the cover design has been finalized and drawn in pencil, black ink can be applied. Always remember to leave enough space in your artwork for the cover type—this is the title of your comic book and any other information you wish to include. The sky on this cover could have been inked in solid black, which would also have been dramatic. However, this would have left very little room for color. Use bold line work to make your drawing punchy and powerful. Remember, this cover has to grab attention!

STEP 4: COLORS

Here we have the final hero cover, in color. Color is especially important on your cover artwork as it will catch your reader's eye. You can achieve this effect by using marker pens, inks, or watercolors. We have chosen to keep the color palette simple, sticking to white and shades of blue and yellow.

LIGHT SOURCES

The first thing to keep in mind as you start to apply color is the light source. In this image there are several: the moon, the street lights, and the office-building windows.

HEROIC HUES

The main body of the hero's costume is a very pale blue. Royal blue has been used for the cape, mask, and gloves. Slightly darker shades of blue have been applied for shading.

MOONLIGHT

The moon itself has been left in white and acts as the perfect bright frame for the main character.

STREET LIGHTS

Yellow tones have been added to establish the second light source. They are applied to create highlights on the gargoyle and to emphasize some outer areas of the hero's figure.

THE STORY COVER

WHAT HAPPENS NEXT?

The story cover attracts the attention of the reader by giving a glimpse of the story inside the comic book. Usually, it's the most exciting part of the plot that makes it onto this type of cover. This cover entices the reader into reading the comic book, to find out the rest of the story.

STEP 1: ROUGHS

In these two thumbnail roughs, our hero is in deep trouble. The question is: which image do you think will make readers most excited?

FIRST ROUGH

Here a supervillain has our hero on the ropes. Can Omegaman possibly defeat such a powerful foe? Showing the hero in pitched battle always makes for an exciting comic book cover.

SECOND ROUGH

In this alternate cover, the stakes have been raised. Now the supervillain has seemingly defeated the hero. The hero has been deliberately made to look small and lifeless in comparison to the maniacal monster. Will Omegaman survive to fight another day? This type of dramatic cover makes the reader eager to buy the comic book to find out what happens next!

STEP 2: PENCILS

We've decided to use the second rough as the basis for our final cover since it feels more shocking. The focal point is the villain, who is almost filling the page, forcing the hero towards the edge. Notice that we have changed the direction in which the hero is facing, so he looks down and away from the villain, making him appear truly defeated.

STEP 3: INKS

When inking the two characters, use a variety of different line thicknesses to prevent the drawing from looking flat. Keep your ink work clean and avoid overworking the drawing by adding unnecessary detail. The buildings don't play a significant part in this composition, so they can be inked solidly in black, with the windows left white. As with the hero cover, the sky has been left blank so there is room to add color.

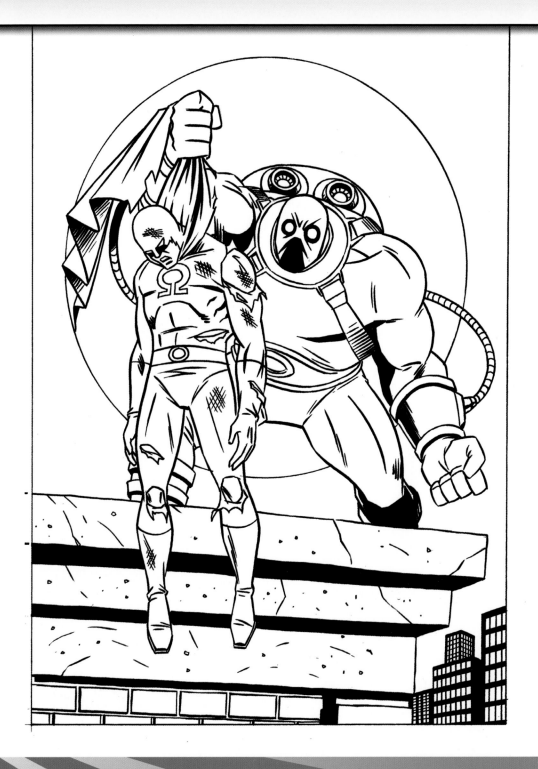

STEP 4: COLORS

This image has been colored using markers, layering darker colors over pale ones. The mainly purple color palette is simple but dramatic.

INDIGO SKY

First, a bold purple is applied to the sky to set the nighttime scene. Leaving the moon as a white disk creates a spotlight effect and leaves you free to use strong colors for the hero and villain.

HIGHLIGHTS

Highlights are added to the monster's suit to show how it reflects the moonlight. Yellow tones are used to create the glow of streetlights on the wall of the building beneath the characters.

CRIMINAL COLORS

The monster is colored by applying light blue followed by layers of lavender gray. These colors create the base color of its suit. Cadmium yellow is used for the metallic parts of the suit. Cool gray is used for the monster's boots.

THE TEASER COVER

WHAT'S GOING ON?

The teaser cover is used in a similar way to the story cover, to give the reader a taste of what to expect within the pages of the comic book. The difference is that the teaser intentionally leaves out some information so the reader must fill in the gaps using his or her own imagination.

STEP 1: ROUGHS

Once again, we tried two different approaches before settling on a favorite.

FIRST ROUGH

A muscular arm holds aloft an emblem torn from the hero's costume. It is left to the reader to guess what has happened. Does this mean that Omegaman has been defeated? Has he in fact survived the confrontation?

SECOND ROUGH

Here the villain is deliberately shown from an unusual angle and cast in shadow. This creates a sense of mystery. Readers might be able to figure out the identity of the villain by looking closely at the details on his outfit, but they'll have to work a little harder than if they were looking at a hero or a story cover.

STEP 2: PENCILS

This final cover may be simple in terms of the amount of detail shown, but the perspective makes it look very different to the usual fight scene. The low angle and heavy use of shading make it appear that the villain is an enormous dark presence looming over the hero.

STEP 3: INKS

You'll need plenty of ink for this cover composition! The villain is shaded almost completely in solid black and the hero is partly obscured by the position of the villain's leg. In this example, the inking stage is almost the most important one as there's very little space left for color. Despite its simplicity, this cover design will be powerful and dramatic.

STEP 4: COLORING

As this is a simple composition with a lot of heavily inked areas, the color palette must be carefully chosen to produce the most exciting effect.

RED LIGHT SPELLS DANGER

We have chosen to use a bright, attention-grabbing red background for our teaser cover, which will contrast dramatically with the black ink. Also, as we're not showing any detail in the background, we can choose a color that's symbolic of the action. Red is often used to alert the reader to potential danger. It's the perfect backdrop for the battle between our hero and villain.

Here are some questions to ask yourself as you design a cover.

- Will your cover design grab the reader's attention?
- Have you left enough space in which to add the type?
- Do your colors work together and do they reflect the message you want to communicate?

HORROR AND MANGA COVERS

OTHER APPROACHES TO COVER DESIGN

The three covers that we have created so far have all drawn on superhero conventions, and all have used the same step-by-step process. Over the next few pages we will showcase some other approaches to cover design.

STEP 1: ROUGH COMPOSITION

Having already figured out the look of the central character, this artist has experimented with different simple shapes for the cover composition. The image on the left has a single large spiral shape curling in towards the monster. The image on the right is broken up by jagged and pointed shapes. Which do you think works best?

STEP 2: ROUGH COLORS

For this second stage, the artist has roughed up a small thumbnail of the color image to make sure that the colors he has chosen work well together. He could make several of these to see which works best.

STEP 3: FINISHED COVER

Now that the artist has decided the composition and colors, he goes through the usual steps of penciling, inking, and coloring the cover.

CREATING A SENSE OF SPEED AND MOVEMENT

This artist wants to make us feel like a martial artist manga character is leaping out of the page right towards the reader. The cover type will appear at the bottom.

normal perspective

downwards perspective

upwards perspective
(The red dot shows the vanishing point,
where the lines of perspective meet.)

STEP 1: ROUGH COMPOSITION

The artist has mapped out lines of perspective with a ruler and placed a high-kicking character in various different positions over them. After careful consideration, he decides that the bottom left image has the best sense of movement and drama.

STEP 2: ROUGH COLORS

One way of making it seem that a still image is moving is to use a technique called speed lines. These lines give us the sense that the background is blurring as we watch an object in the foreground moving at great speed. The speed lines here follow the same lines of perspective as the rest of the objects in the room. The martial artist's vivid red suit has been chosen to make her stand out against the calm background colors.

STEP 3: FINISHED COVER

Here is the final inked and colored cover image. As a finishing touch, the artist has used yet another technique for showing speed. This is called after images. These images follow behind the character like echoes. The idea is that they make it seem that the character is moving so fast that you can barely keep track of where they are.

GLOSSARY

color palette (KUH-lur PA-let) A selection of colors that have been chosen for a picture.

composition (kom-puh-ZIH-shun) How the elements of an artwork or a comic book page are arranged to make them look appealing.

layering (LAY-er-ing) Placing objects or colors over each other.

light source (LYT SAWRS) Where the light in a picture is coming from, such as a street lamp. The source itself might not be included in the picture.

manga (MAHN-guh) A style of comic book and animation that first appeared in Japan.

martial artist (MAHR-shul AHR-tist) An expert in a skillful fighting sport such as kung fu.

perspective (per-SPEK-tiv) A way of drawing items so that they look correctly sized and shaped in relation to each other and in relation to the point from which they are being viewed.

thumbnail (THUM-nayl) A small, rough sketch.

tone (TOHN) A shade of a color, such as light blue or dark green.

type (TYP) Text that appears in books, comics, or newspapers. The type on the cover of a graphic novel usually includes the title and the name of the author.